DISCARDED

398.2   Wildsmith, Brian
W   The hare and the tortoise; pictures by
        Brian Wildsmith; based on the fable by La
        Fontaine.   New York, Watts, F., 1966.
            unp. illus. col. draws.

c.1

MORGAN HILL UNIFIED SCHOOL DIST.
   JACKSON MEDIA CENTER

1. Animals-Stories 2. Fables 3. Folklore
I. Title

First published 1966 by Oxford University Press
First American Publication 1967 by Franklin Watts, Inc.

Library of Congress Catalog Card Number: AC67–10019
Printed in Austria

PICTURES BY *Brian Wildsmith*

BASED ON THE FABLE BY LA FONTAINE

The Hare and the Tortoise

watts
international

FRANKLIN WATTS, INC.
845 THIRD AVENUE, NEW YORK, N.Y. 10022

A hare and a tortoise were having an argument. The hare, who could run very fast, thought he was much more clever than the tortoise, who could only move slowly and had to carry his house around on his back.

But the tortoise did not agree. To the hare's surprise the tortoise challenged him to a race. "We will run from here, over the hill, through the hedge, then along the carrot field to the old cart," he said. The hare laughed. "I am sure to win, but we will race if you like."

News of the race spread quickly, and the birds and animals gathered to watch.

"The tortoise will not have a chance!" cried the fox.
"Wait and see," said the owl.

The cock offered to start the race. The spectators stood back, and the cock swelled up ready to give the signal.

"Cock-a-doodle-doo!" In a flash the hare was off, flying over the grass. The tortoise had hardly moved.

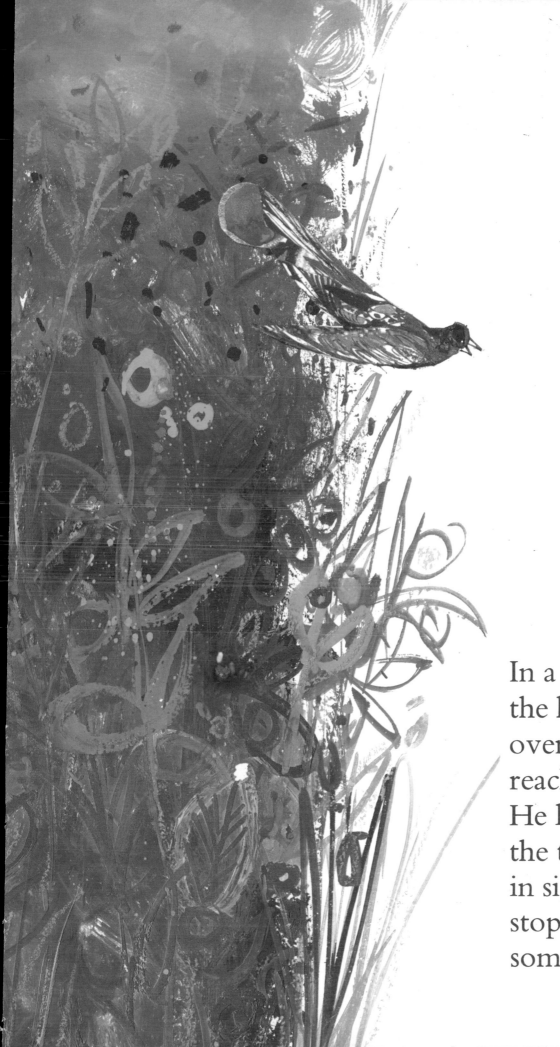

In a few moments
the hare had run
over the hill and
reached the hedge.
He looked behind, but
the tortoise was not
in sight. The hare
stopped to nibble
some tasty leaves.

The tortoise plodded on, and came to the hill. It was hard work for him to climb it, and the birds called encouragement to help him on his way.

The hare had finished eating the leaves in the hedge and dashed off again at full speed to the carrot field. He was very fond of carrots and could not resist stopping to eat some.

He ate and ate until he was
so full he had to lie down and sleep
for a while.

The tortoise had only just reached the hedge.

He was already tired, but kept walking slowly on.

At last he reached the carrot field, but the hare was too fast asleep to notice him passing by.

Suddenly the hare woke up. He stared in astonishment towards the old cart, the winning post. The tortoise was almost there!

The hare ran as fast as he could but it was no use —the tortoise had won the race!

All the animals gathered round the tortoise while he told how, in his slow and steady way, he had won the race from the quick and careless hare.